Flip

SCHOLASTIC BOOK SERVICES

NEW YORK • LONDON • RICHMOND HILL, ONTARIO

Flip

By WESLEY DENNIS

Copyright © 1941, 1962 by Wesley Dennis. This revised edition is published by Scholastic Book Services, a division of Scholastic Magazines, Inc., by arrangement with The Viking Press, Inc.

5th printing .... December 1966

Printed in the U.S.A.

to Linda and Karen

Flip was born.

His home was a large farm.

There were miles and miles of fences and big trees.

A little brook ran through the green fields.

Flip wanted to get out there and play.

Soon his mother was teaching him to walk

and then to run.

Flip thought this was great fun.

When they came to the brook,

Flip's mother would jump lightly over it.

Then she would jump back again.

Flip wished he could jump over the brook too.

Flip could do plenty of other things.

He could kick and buck.

He could run circles around his mother.

Sometimes he nipped her and pulled her tail.

Then his mother would jump over the brook

to get away.

Flip wished he could jump across the brook

like that.

He tried and tried.

Sometimes he would run right up to the brook

and then stop.

Sometimes he did not stop soon enough.

And then he would fall in.

When he did jump, he always landed

in the water.

Now there was only one thing in the world

that Flip wanted.

He wanted to jump that brook.

One day he jumped so hard and so long

that he tired himself out.

And he fell asleep wishing —

wishing that he could jump the brook

the way his mother did.

While he was sleeping, he had a dream.

In his dream, he felt something on his shoulders.

He looked around.

He had grown a pair of beautiful

silvery wings.

He was so excited that his hair stood on end.

He thought, "With these wings

I can jump over anything!

I can jump over that haystack."

And he did! Now he did not want to stop.

On and on he went, over the fences.

He went higher and higher.

Now he could say "Hello" to the iron horse

that told the way the wind was blowing.

Flip was sorry for him.

The iron horse could only go around and around.

Flip could fly anywhere.

This was fun — more fun than he ever had before.

He wanted only one thing more.

He wanted his friends on the farm

to see him jumping — jumping higher

than any horse ever jumped before.

So he swooped down over the barn.

The pig saw him coming, and he was so scared

that his tail stood straight up,

and stayed that way.

When old Mother Hen saw the flying horse,

she thought the world was coming to an end.

She ran to the nearest sunflower

and called to her chicks.

The cat jumped on the back of the goat

to see better.

But the goat was so scared that he ran BANG

into the fence.

Meow! The cat went sailing through the air.

Flip was having great fun.

But he did wish that big horsefly

would leave him alone.

But it didn't leave him alone.

So Flip snapped at it.

As he moved, he woke up.

And there, right in front of him,

was the same brook that he had tried

so many times to jump.

It would be easy now with his silver wings!

So he backed up to get a good running start —

And he jumped right over the brook!

He was so happy!

He looked back to admire once again

his silver wings.

They were gone!

GREAT SCOTT — He had jumped the brook

without wings!